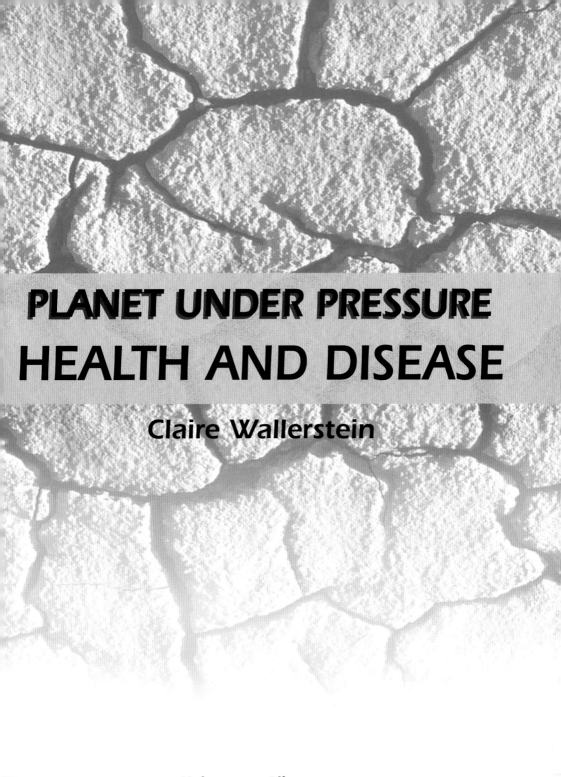

PLANET UNDER PRESSURE
HEALTH AND DISEASE

Claire Wallerstein

Heinemann Library
Chicago, Illinois

© 2007 Heinemann Library
a division of Reed Elsevier Inc.
Chicago, Illinois

Customer Service 888-454-2279

Visit our website at www.heinemannlibrary.com

Designed by Monkey Puzzle and Jane Hawkins
Printed in China by South China Printing Company

11 10 09 08 07
10 9 8 7 6 5 4 3 2 1

Library of Congress Cataloging-in-Publication Data
Wallerstein, Claire, 1969-
    Health and disease / Claire Wallerstein.
        p. cm. -- (Planet under pressure)
    Includes bibliographical references and index.
    ISBN-13: 978-1-4034-8215-0 (lib. bdg. (hardcover))
    ISBN-10: 1-4034-8215-2 (lib. bdg. (hardcover))
    1. Environmental health--Juvenile literature. I. Title.
    RA566.235W35 2006
    616.9'8--dc22
                                        2006017849

Acknowledgments
The author and publisher are grateful to the following for permission to reproduce copyright
material: Corbis pp. 9 (Owen Franken), 16 (Tom Stewart); Getty Images
pp. 7 (Photographer's Choice), 10 (Hulton Archive), 14 (Stone), 17 (Stone), 20 (AFP), 24 (Taxi),
26 (Image Bank), 30 (Hulton Archive), 31, 32, 34 (Taxi), 36 (Stone), 37 (Stone), 38, 39 (AFP), 41
(AFP); Barry Lewis/Sight Savers p. 18; Panos Pictures pp. 29 (Penny Tweedie), 40 (Giacomo
Pirozzi); Reuters p. 35; Science Photo Library pp. 8 (Jackie Lewin, Royal Free Hospital), 12 (AJ
Photo/Hop Americain), 28 (CDC); Still Pictures pp. 13 (Matt Meadows), 21 (Ron Giling), 23
(Jorgen Schytte). Maps and graphs by Martin Darlison at Encompass Graphics.

Cover photograph of an operating theater reproduced with permission of Alamy (Dynamic
Graphics Group/IT Stock Free) and of a health care clinic in Tanzania with
permission of Still Pictures (Jorgen Schytte).

Contents

Any words appearing in the text in bold,
like this, are explained in the Glossary.

Malnutrition Around the World

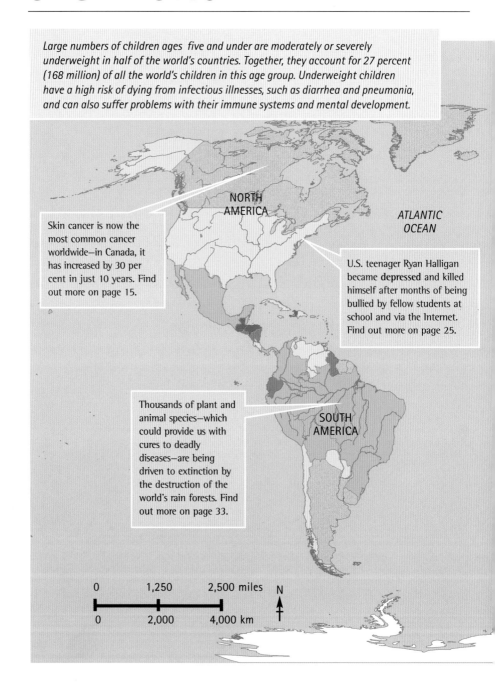

Large numbers of children ages five and under are moderately or severely underweight in half of the world's countries. Together, they account for 27 percent (168 million) of all the world's children in this age group. Underweight children have a high risk of dying from infectious illnesses, such as diarrhea and pneumonia, and can also suffer problems with their immune systems and mental development.

NORTH AMERICA

ATLANTIC OCEAN

Skin cancer is now the most common cancer worldwide—in Canada, it has increased by 30 per cent in just 10 years. Find out more on page 15.

U.S. teenager Ryan Halligan became **depressed** and killed himself after months of being bullied by fellow students at school and via the Internet. Find out more on page 25.

Thousands of plant and animal species—which could provide us with cures to deadly diseases—are being driven to extinction by the destruction of the world's rain forests. Find out more on page 33.

SOUTH AMERICA

| 0 | 1,250 | 2,500 miles |
| 0 | 2,000 | 4,000 km |

N

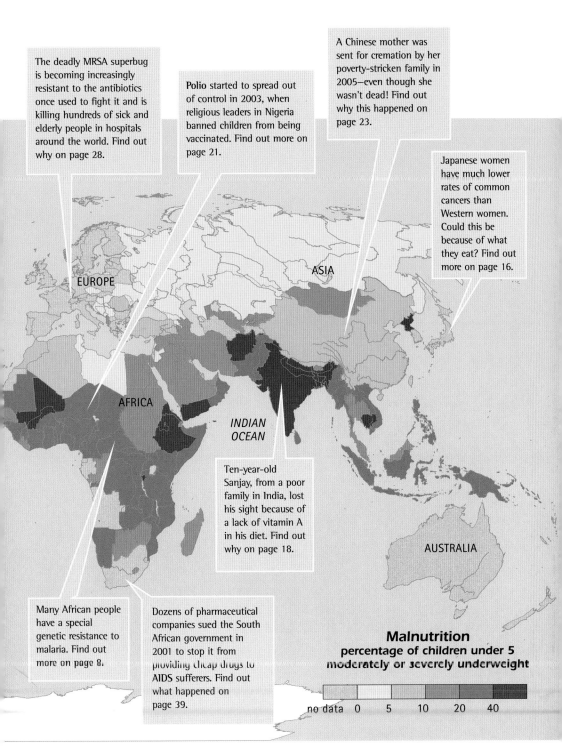

The deadly MRSA superbug is becoming increasingly resistant to the antibiotics once used to fight it and is killing hundreds of sick and elderly people in hospitals around the world. Find out why on page 28.

Polio started to spread out of control in 2003, when religious leaders in Nigeria banned children from being vaccinated. Find out more on page 21.

A Chinese mother was sent for cremation by her poverty-stricken family in 2005—even though she wasn't dead! Find out why this happened on page 23.

Japanese women have much lower rates of common cancers than Western women. Could this be because of what they eat? Find out more on page 16.

EUROPE

ASIA

AFRICA

INDIAN OCEAN

Ten-year-old Sanjay, from a poor family in India, lost his sight because of a lack of vitamin A in his diet. Find out why on page 18.

AUSTRALIA

Many African people have a special genetic resistance to malaria. Find out more on page 8.

Dozens of pharmaceutical companies sued the South African government in 2001 to stop it from providing cheap drugs to AIDS sufferers. Find out what happened on page 39.

Malnutrition
percentage of children under 5
moderately or severely underweight

no data   0   5   10   20   40

Source: State of the World Atlas

The Health of the World

One of the best ways of measuring people's health is to look at how long they live. Today, people around the world can expect to live, on average, 63 years—in 1900, the average was just 30 years. However, there are big differences between countries. Life expectancy in Andorra is the world's longest at 83.5 years, while in Zambia it is just 32.4 years.

Life expectancy is an average figure, because some people live longer than others. It will be low if a country has a high infant mortality rate (the number of babies dying before the age of one). In wealthy Singapore, where life expectancy is 80 years, only 2.3 babies die per 1,000 born. In Mozambique, 135 babies die per 1,000 and life expectancy is only 45 years. If you lived in Mozambique, four pupils sitting in your class today would never have reached their first birthday.

People in poor countries generally get sick and die younger than people in the richer, developed countries because they do not have:

- enough food
- clean drinking water
- access to doctors and modern medicine.

In the developing world, around 18 million people die of starvation each year, and billions more go hungry and have no clean drinking water. Diseases wiped out long ago in the West are still common.

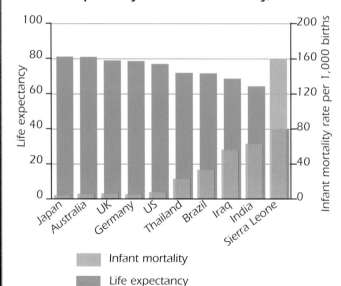

Life expectancy and infant mortality, 2005

Infant mortality

Life expectancy

Source: CIA World Factbook

Food supply is rarely a problem in wealthy countries, however, where many people suffer from diseases caused by eating too much.

GOING BACKWARD INSTEAD OF FORWARD

In some countries, people's health is getting worse, not better. In Botswana, more than one in three adults is infected with **HIV/AIDS**. Life expectancy has plunged from 67 years in 1985 to just 34 years today. Many former **Communist** countries fell into poverty after the 1991 collapse of the **Soviet Union**. **Depression**, drug and alcohol abuse, HIV/AIDS, and **tuberculosis (TB)** have all risen dramatically, while health services have broken down. Male life expectancy in Russia has fallen from 70 years in 1987 to 61 years today.

DIFFERENT WAYS OF TREATING ILLNESS

In developed countries, most people have access to good health care (doctors, hospitals, and medicines), but this is not the case in much of the world.

Eight out of ten people worldwide, mostly in poor countries, still rely on traditional healers, such as witch doctors—often because there are very few doctors, or medicines are too expensive. In Tanzania, the government spends only $4 per person per year on health care, compared with $1,500 in Australia.

However, some traditional therapies, such as **acupuncture** from China and **ayurveda** from India, work well for some conditions. Developed thousands of years ago, these therapies are often used in the West to help treat illnesses that still cannot be cured by conventional medicine.

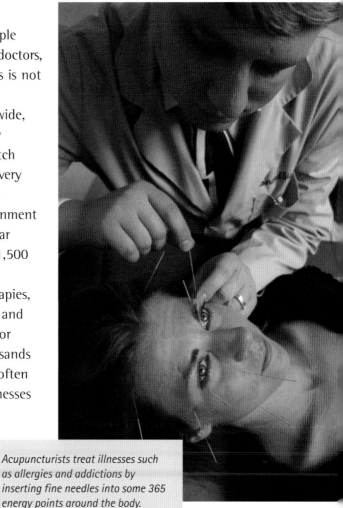

Acupuncturists treat illnesses such as allergies and addictions by inserting fine needles into some 365 energy points around the body.

In sickness and in health

Disease-causing **viruses, bacteria,** and parasites are constantly trying to get into our bodies through dirty food or water, insect bites, open wounds, and by other means. Our bodies usually manage to fight them off. However, if germs get a foothold, they may breed rapidly.

Some even alter our behavior to spread themselves further—for example, colds make people sneeze, while rabies makes dogs bite other animals.

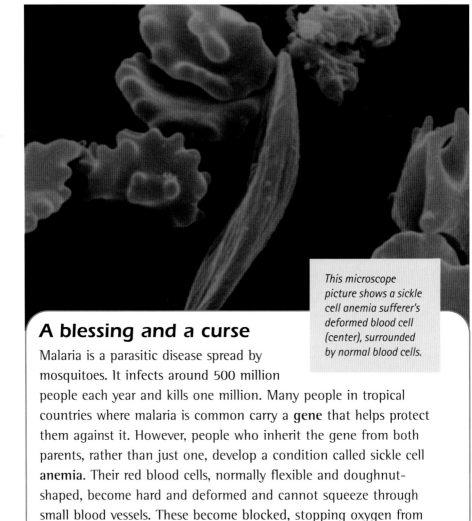

This microscope picture shows a sickle cell anemia sufferer's deformed blood cell (center), surrounded by normal blood cells.

A blessing and a curse

Malaria is a parasitic disease spread by mosquitoes. It infects around 500 million people each year and kills one million. Many people in tropical countries where malaria is common carry a **gene** that helps protect them against it. However, people who inherit the gene from both parents, rather than just one, develop a condition called sickle cell **anemia**. Their red blood cells, normally flexible and doughnut-shaped, become hard and deformed and cannot squeeze through small blood vessels. These become blocked, stopping oxygen from getting to where it is needed, causing severe pain, organ damage, and even early death.

Once infected, our immune systems go into action, with the lymph glands like those in our neck or armpits producing billions of white blood cells to hunt down and destroy invaders. We may develop a fever to make our bodies too hot for microbes, or vomit to get rid of them. Our bodies also make antibodies that can recognize the microbe and destroy it if it tries to attack again.

Although some infectious diseases are too serious for our bodies to cure alone, many can be treated with medicines.

If a disease infects many people at the same time, it is called an epidemic. A pandemic is a disease, such as AIDS, that quickly spreads to affect much of the world.

When the bugs win

People who have never been exposed to an illness before suffer much more if infected. For example, thousands of Native Americans, who had no antibodies against the common cold, died from this apparently "harmless" illness after European explorers arrived in the 1400s.

Microbes constantly change their shape, tricking our defenses, and our immune systems may be unable to fight them off if we are very tired, stressed, or have other health problems.

Diseases from within

Non-infectious diseases, for example cancer or heart disease, are often caused by eating badly, smoking, or not getting enough exercise. Some people's genes may also make them more likely to get such diseases.

Other diseases, such as **cystic fibrosis**, can only be caused by faulty genes.

Mental Illnesses, such as depression or **schizophrenia**, can also be caused by a mixture of problems in sufferers' lives—for example, trauma or grief— and their genes.

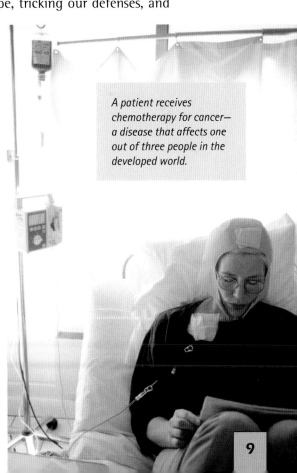

A patient receives chemotherapy for cancer— a disease that affects one out of three people in the developed world.

9

Health and Disease Throughout the Ages

In the Stone Age, people lived in small **nomadic** tribes and ate a varied diet of meat, insects, fruits, and vegetables. However, life was tough and dangerous, and many died of starvation in lean times. Nearly everyone had parasites such as worms, and life expectancy was only about 25 years.

Health in the ancient world

Around 10,000 years ago, people started to tame animals and grow cereal crops, which could be stored. This secure food supply allowed the human population to grow and the first towns to develop. However, people's diet —mainly cereals, such as wheat, with only a little milk and meat—was very poor.

Close contact with livestock in very dirty and crowded conditions led to some animal diseases infecting humans. Influenza (the flu) was originally a disease of pigs and ducks, while measles, tuberculosis (TB), and smallpox all came from cattle. These diseases, combined with malnutrition, saw life expectancy fall even lower than in the Stone Age.

Later, as people started to travel, their diseases traveled with them. An efficient road network stretching to the furthest corners of the Roman Empire allowed deadly plagues to travel huge distances within days, killing millions.

The Black Death, arriving along trade routes from Asia, killed 25 percent of Europe's population in the 1100s —in a similar way as AIDS is today spreading along trucking routes in Africa.

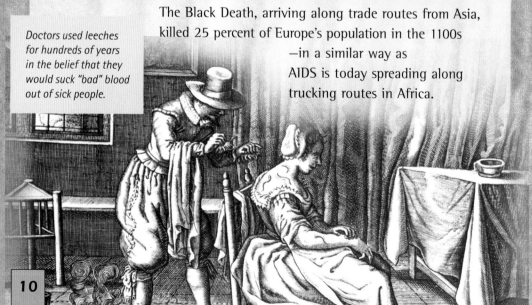

Doctors used leeches for hundreds of years in the belief that they would suck "bad" blood out of sick people.

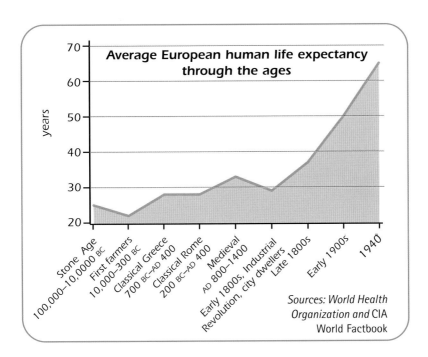

Average European human life expectancy through the ages

Sources: World Health Organization and CIA World Factbook

DEADLY MISTAKES

For thousands of years, people did not understand the true causes of diseases, often thinking they were caused by witchcraft, imbalances in the body, or the planets. The flu (influenza), for example, was thought to be under the "influence" of the stars.

Some of these beliefs were held until the 1800s, largely because the Church banned medical research, such as **autopsies**, which could have taught people more about how the body really worked.

Some ancient treatments were very effective, however, and are still used today. Aspirin, which comes from willow bark, was used by the ancient Greeks. However, many other treatments, such as "bleeding" people—removing large amounts of their blood—were often useless, or even deadly.

GONE FOREVER?

Some diseases have disappeared or are now very rare. Smallpox, for example, once killed hundreds of thousands of people a year and left millions more blind, deaf, or horribly scarred. It was completely wiped out in 1977 following a worldwide vaccination campaign. However, samples are still kept for scientific research. In fact, the last victim died after the disease escaped from a laboratory in Birmingham, United Kingdom, in 1978. Some people fear that terrorists could get their hands on these samples and unleash a worldwide epidemic.

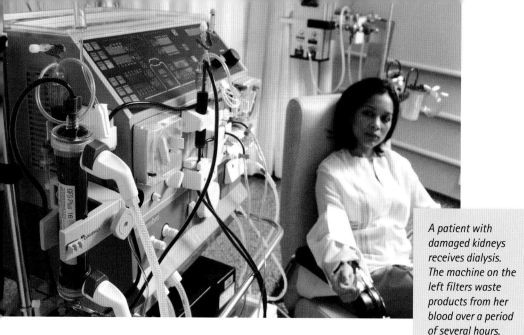

A patient with damaged kidneys receives dialysis. The machine on the left filters waste products from her blood over a period of several hours.

The war on disease

Human health—in the developed world, at least—has improved dramatically over the past century or two. Life expectancy in U.S. cities, for example, rose from just 30 years in 1800 to 49 in 1901 and 77 in 2004.

THE WATER CONNECTION

During the Industrial Revolution of the early 1800s, thousands of people moved to the cities to work in factories. Epidemics raged in the dirty, overcrowded conditions, killing hundreds of thousands of people. Even the rich didn't escape—Queen Victoria's husband Albert died of **typhoid** in 1861.

People didn't understand that disease was spread by sewage-polluted water until a London doctor noticed that many victims of an 1854 **cholera** outbreak were using the same water pump. When he removed the pump handle to prevent them from using it, the death rate plummeted.

MIRACLE IN A COWSHED

In the 1790s, a doctor named Edward Jenner found that milkmaids often suffered from cowpox, a mild illness affecting cattle, but were later **immune** to smallpox. Jenner rubbed cowpox pus into a scratch on an eight-year-old boy's arm and later deliberately infected him with smallpox. The boy was immune—his body had learned how to fight both the cowpox virus and the closely-related smallpox one.

This paved the way for vaccinations against many other diseases, which today save four million lives each year. The word vaccination comes from *vacca*—the Latin word for cow.

THE TECHNOLOGICAL REVOLUTION

Scientific progress over the past century has also improved health dramatically, including:

- The first organ transplant in 1953. Today, transplantation saves 80,000 lives each year in the United States alone.
- Pasteurization—heating foods such as milk to kill harmful bacteria.
- Dialysis, a machine that does the work of patients' diseased kidneys by cleaning their blood.
- X-rays, discovered in 1895, allowing doctors to see patients' bones for the first time, while MRI (magnetic resonance imaging), developed in the 1980s, provides detailed images of soft tissue, such as the brain.
- Some babies can now survive after just 24 weeks in the womb (a normal pregnancy lasts 40 weeks) thanks to incubator technology, which keeps them warm, feeds them, and helps them breathe.

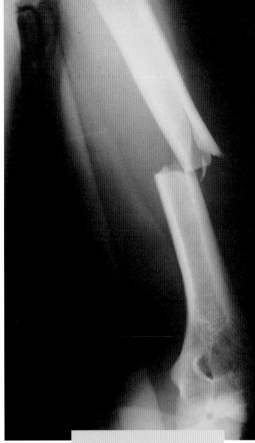

This X-ray picture clearly shows the break in a patient's upper arm and will allow doctors to fix the injury properly.

HELP FROM WAR AND SPACE

Some medical advances have even come about thanks to wars and space exploration. Antibiotics, for example, were developed in World War II (1939–1945) to treat soldiers' infected wounds. These have since saved millions of lives. In the Iraq War, dramatic breakthroughs have been made in blood clotting products to stop injured soldiers from bleeding to death.

Meanwhile, astronauts' spacesuit technology has allowed the development of special clothing to help people suffering from conditions that make their bodies react dangerously to sunlight.

Health Today

The developed world

The most serious diseases in the developed world include cancer, heart disease, stroke, and diabetes. These are largely caused by the fact that our bodies are still designed to suit Stone Age conditions—but our lifestyle and diet are not.

- Most people spend several hours a day watching television and take the bus or car to school or work. Lack of exercise contributes to **obesity** and heart disease.
- Tobacco kills one in every two smokers, and will be the leading cause of death worldwide by 2030.
- Alcohol and drugs can cause mental illnesses and some cancers. Liver **cirrhosis** is one of the ten leading causes of death in the United States.
- The stresses of modern life, such as school, work, or relationships may cause depression, the world's fastest-growing health problem.

A boy uses an asthma inhaler to help him breathe—something that is now part of everyday life for millions of children worldwide.

Sun, sea, sand, . . . and cancer

Skin cancer is now the world's most common form of cancer, largely caused by more vacations being taken in the sun. In Canada, it has risen 30 percent in just 10 years, with almost 80,000 people diagnosed in 2004—enough to fill four ice hockey arenas. This is made worse by the fact that 10 percent of Canada's protective ozone layer has been destroyed by **CFCs** and other chemicals. People usually spend more time in the sun as children—when their skin is at greatest risk of sunburn—than in the entire rest of their lives.

Poor people and ethnic minorities in developed countries usually have less access to education, jobs, and health information, and often suffer more from these "lifestyle" diseases. In 2000, aboriginal men in Australia had a life expectancy of only 56 years—over 20 years less than the overall Australian male population.

THE ALLERGY EXPLOSION

Modern city living has gone hand-in-hand with a huge increase in allergies and asthma. In the United States, 4.4 million children under 18 (more than one in 15) are affected with asthma. Each day, 30,000 people have an asthma attack in the United States and 14 of them will die from it. This seems to be linked with air pollution, passive smoking, and even hygiene. Children who grow up in very clean homes and rarely play outdoors hardly ever come into contact with dirt or germs. This may cause their immune systems to overreact to harmless substances, such as dust, tomatoes, or animal fur, later in life. Children who grow up on farms have much lower rates of allergies and asthma.

WHAT DO YOU THINK?
Should smokers, overeaters, and alcoholics be given life-saving medical treatment?

- They brought their health problems upon themselves, knowing the risks. Why should others have to pay to help them?
- They may be smoking, overeating, or drinking to cope with other problems in their lives. It would be cruel not to treat them.

Eating ourselves to death?

Although nearly everyone in the West eats the recommended 2,500 calories per day, these often come from fatty, sugary, salt-laden foods. Some people are actually malnourished, as they do not get enough vitamins and minerals from this kind of diet. In the United States, 64 percent of the population (including 40 percent of children) is now overweight or obese. Only 60 percent of obese people live to be 60—compared to 90 percent of those of normal weight.

The answer in Asia?

Lung, breast, and colon cancer are the most common cancers among Western women, but were until recently very rare in Japan, where people have traditionally eaten much less fat and more fish, vegetables, and rice. The link with diet was clearly shown when, between 1950 and 1975, these cancers doubled or even tripled among Japanese women. This occurred at the same time as they started to eat much more meat and dairy products, while rice consumption fell by 70 percent.

Poor diet is responsible for:

- Up to 35 percent of cancers. One in three people in developed countries get cancer—more than twice the rate for developing countries.
- Heart disease—the biggest killer in developed countries. It kills someone every 34 seconds in the United States.
- Type 2 diabetes, until recently only found in overweight adults. Now growing fast among children in developed countries, diabetes can cause blindness, kidney failure, and serious circulation problems. Diabetics are also very likely to suffer from heart disease.
- Stroke—forecast to be the world's major cause of disability by 2020. Caused by blood supply being blocked to the brain, strokes kill brain cells, often causing paralysis and problems with sight, memory, speech, and understanding.

Many processed foods—often targeted at children—contain additives, such as sodium nitrite and hydrogenated fats, which have been linked to heart attacks, strokes, and cancer.

People in Mediterranean countries, such as Italy and France, tend to eat less of these processed foods than people in the United States and some European countries. They have a healthier diet including fresh fruit, fish, and olive oil, and have lower rates of some cancers and heart disease.

What can you do?

- Eat no more than 2,500 calories per day, including five portions of fruit and vegetables.
- Drink 8 glasses of water per day (2 liters).
- Keep active for 30 minutes five times a week. Just walking to school or using stairs instead of elevators can make a difference.
- Eat a balanced diet rather than relying on vitamin supplements to compensate for eating junk food.
- Maintain a healthy weight. Frequent dieting can have a negative effect because your body stores more fat in case of another "famine!"

Eating a healthy diet, including five portions of fruit or vegetables each day, could help to prevent many life-threatening diseases.

Blinded by hunger

Ten-year-old Sanjay from Gujarat, India, went blind at the age of two

because of a lack of vitamin A in his diet. Sanjay's parents are extremely poor and do not own any land, so the family often have little to eat but rice. Vitamin A is found in milk, fish, liver, and dark-colored vegetables. A British charity is now teaching Sanjay how to look after himself and read Braille, and his friend Kishan helps him get around the village. However, he will never recover his sight. Lack of vitamin A needlessly blinds 500,000 children each year.

Sanjay (right), who was left blind for life by malnutrition, is helped around the village by his friend, Kishan.

Disease in the developing world

Tragically, many common diseases in the developing world stem from poverty and could easily be prevented or cured.

- Diarrhea kills around 2.2 million people, mostly children, each year through severe **dehydration.**
- Malaria kills an African child every 30 seconds. Death rates have doubled in the past 20 years.
- Lung diseases, such as **pneumonia** and tuberculosis, kill more than 6 million people per year.
- Almost 40 million people are infected with **HIV**, and more than 3 million die of AIDS each year, 70 percent of them in Africa.
- Parasites, such as worms (which infect 2 billion people), can cause weight loss, anemia, learning difficulties, and organ failure.

People already weak from hunger, or in dirty refugee camps, are at great risk. In Sudan, Africa, around 200,000 people died from disease and starvation during the 2004 civil war.

Another problem is that two-thirds of the developing world's medical graduates leave to seek better pay abroad, creating doctor shortages in their home countries. Meanwhile, 10 percent of medicines sold in the developing world are fakes, made by criminal gangs. These waste sick people's money and may even kill them.

THE WORST OF BOTH WORLDS

By 2025, 90 percent of the world's city dwellers will live in poorer countries. While many will continue to suffer malnutrition and infectious diseases, "Western" illnesses will also increase as lifestyles change.

For example, more and more people in poorer countries now smoke. Tobacco shops in Morocco increased from 9,600 in 1969 to 20,000 in 2003. By 2020, seven out of every ten people dying from smoking will be in the developing world.

Health problems will also grow as people eat more Western junk foods. In Samoa, for example, 80 percent of men are now obese. In sketches drawn when the first Europeans arrived in the late 1700s, no Samoan men were overweight.

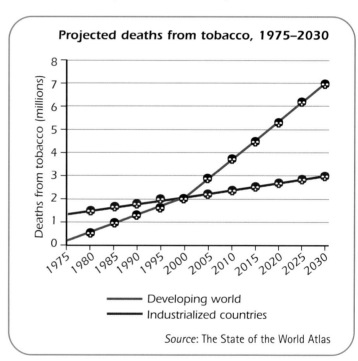

Projected deaths from tobacco, 1975–2030

Deaths from tobacco (millions)

—— Developing world
—— Industrialized countries

Source: The State of the World Atlas

What can you do?

- Read more about the causes of health problems in the developing world.
- Raise funds to help organizations working to help the sick in the developing world, for example, by holding a garage sale or getting involved in a sponsored event.

Impacts of World Health Patterns

A pinprick that protects millions

Diseases such as typhoid and diphtheria were major killers until recently in the developed world, but are now hardly heard of, thanks to vaccinations. Vaccinations also save millions of lives in the developing world. Many countries have held mass immunization days—for example, China vaccinated 83 million children against **polio** in just two days in 1994!

However, vaccination can be costly, and some poor countries may divert funds away to seemingly bigger problems, such as AIDS, when a disease seems to be "almost" wiped out. Other children can be hard to reach. Immunization programs collapsed during the Afghanistan war in the 1990s. Fewer than four in ten Afghan children are now vaccinated against measles, and the country has the world's second highest death rate from this illness.

In fact, less than 70 percent of children worldwide today receive immunization against the most common diseases. This is very dangerous because unless at least 90 percent of children are vaccinated, diseases can flare up again.

A baby in East Timor, Asia, is vaccinated against measles, a disease that can sometimes cause deafness, convulsions, mental retardation, or even death.

WORKING FOR GLOBAL IMMUNITY

The Global Alliance for Vaccines and Immunization (GAVI) was set up in 2000 by international governments, charities, vaccine manufacturers, and other bodies. It provides funding to ensure 90 percent vaccination coverage worldwide by 2015, which will save 10 million lives in 72 countries.

Vaccination programs will also be used to provide other effective, cheap health products, including vitamin supplements and insecticide-sprayed bed nets to prevent malaria mosquitoes from biting children while they sleep— potentially saving millions more lives.

GAVI's work will cost $2.2 billion, but this will be money well spent. Although diseases such as polio are not now found in the developed world, Western countries still pay millions of dollars each year to vaccinate their children against them. International air travel allows diseases to cross huge distances quickly, so vaccination programs cannot stop anywhere in the world until a disease is totally wiped out.

The polio problem

In 2003, some Nigerian Islamic leaders claimed the United States had deliberately contaminated polio vaccines to make their children sterile, as part of the war on terrorism. Many regions in northern Nigeria —one of only six pockets of naturally occurring polio left on Earth—stopped immunizing children altogether.

As a result, this strain of polio spread to at least 10 other African countries, including Botswana over 2,500 miles (4,000 km) away, and Indonesia in Southeast Asia. Many of these countries had been free from polio for years. Although immunizations have now started again in Nigeria, it is expected to cost at least $150 million to bring the disease back under control, and international plans to completely wipe out polio have been set back.

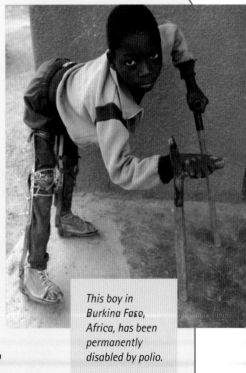

This boy in Burkina Faso, Africa, has been permanently disabled by polio.

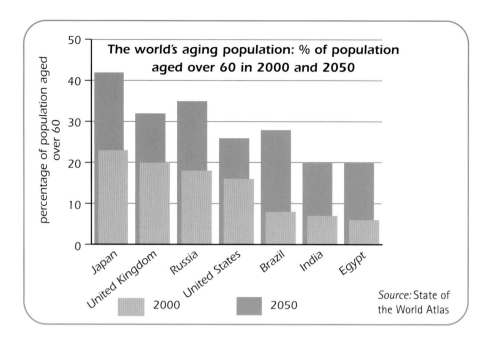

The world's aging population: % of population aged over 60 in 2000 and 2050

Source: State of the World Atlas

2000   2050

Counting the cost...

Good, free health care is something people take for granted in most developed countries. However, as people live longer and longer, these health systems are becoming over-burdened, because elderly people have many more health problems than the young. Younger people may soon have to start paying more taxes, or retiring later to provide enough funds to keep national health services afloat.

A different system in the United States means the government provides free health care only for the very poorest and the elderly. Most people pay for private health insurance to cover their medical care. However, over 40 million Americans are not insured, either because they cannot afford it or because they choose not to. They often do not seek help until a medical condition becomes an emergency, and this may lead to them dying young.

PREVENTION IS BETTER THAN CURE

Many of today's most common diseases require very expensive treatment. Herceptin, a new drug for breast cancer, costs $40,000 per patient per year, while open heart surgery costs around $60,000. Many countries now run preventive medicine campaigns, educating people about diet and exercise. Some, including Canada and India, have also banned the advertising of tobacco products. These campaigns will save governments huge amounts of money if they mean less people get sick.

A roadside billboard in Zambia. African countries urge people to use condoms rather than risk being infected with HIV by having unsafe sex.

THE COST OF ILLNESS IN THE DEVELOPING WORLD

Many developing countries provide little or no health care. People may have to sell their homes or belongings to pay for medicines, or simply die without treatment. Children may have to care for a sick parent, or go out to work to support the family, meaning they cannot go to school. As they miss out on education, they usually fall much deeper into poverty. This can affect whole economies, especially in Africa, where 70 percent of the world's HIV-positive people live. As infection rates rise, less people are healthy enough to work—meaning fewer taxes are paid to support health care provision.

African countries need to devote 15 percent of their **GDP** in order to effectively tackle AIDS and other health emergencies, but most have only very small health budgets. Malawi has only 1.6 doctors per 100,000 people, meaning each doctor must look after enough patients to fill a large football stadium. In comparison, Italy has 550 doctors per 100,000.

Left for dead

You Guoying, 47, from China, was sent for cremation in November 2005 following a brain **hemorrhage**—even though she was still alive. She was only saved because the undertaker noticed tears in her eyes. Her family said they had no option because three days of hospital care had cost $1,200—their entire life savings. It is thought that around half of China's farmers now cannot afford health care since full-scale social welfare ended in the 1980s. There have been many suicides among people unable to pay medical bills.

The rise of depression

People today are richer, and live longer than ever—and yet the world's most rapidly growing health problem is depression, set to become the second biggest cause of human illness by 2020.

One in three of us will suffer from depression at some point in our lives, and it is the cause of 30 percent of all days taken off work. Women are affected twice as often as men. For some, depression is so serious that they cannot bear to go on living. Every 40 seconds, a depressed person kills him or herself.

It is not entirely clear why depression is increasing so fast. However, life today is often much more stressful than it was in the past, when most people grew up and died in the same village, doing the same job, surrounded by people they knew.

Today, it can be hard to get a job or earn enough money. Family breakdown is more common, and as people live longer, they may spend many years living with pain or sickness. Issues such as climate change and terrorism also cause anxiety. Many people use drugs, alcohol, or smoke—but addictions can also cause depression.

When people become depressed, they are unable to see any way out of their problems.

What you can do

- If you feel very down for more than two weeks, confide in a friend, family member, teacher, or counselor. This can't make things worse, and may really help.
- Keep active. Exercise releases chemicals in the brain that can improve your state of mind.

Bullied into desperation

Ryan Halligan, 13, from New York, killed himself in 2003 after years of being bullied at school and via the Internet. Ryan, who had some learning difficulties, suffered verbal bullying (other children calling him names and insulting him) but he was not physically hurt, so his parents just advised him to ignore the bullying. Later, lies were spread around school and via Internet messaging that Ryan was gay. Ryan became very depressed. He did not confide in his parents or teachers, and he eventually took his own life.

NOT JUST FOR THE RICH

Depression is also growing rapidly in the developing world. However, 47 percent of the world's countries still have no policies or programs to deal with it.

In Zimbabwe—a country that has recently gone through war, famine, and where more than one in four adults are infected with HIV—there are only 10 psychiatrists for 11 million people. Depression is hard enough to diagnose even in developed countries, as it can have such different symptoms from patient to patient. In the developing world, people often believe it is caused by evil spirits, and sufferers may be too ashamed to seek help.

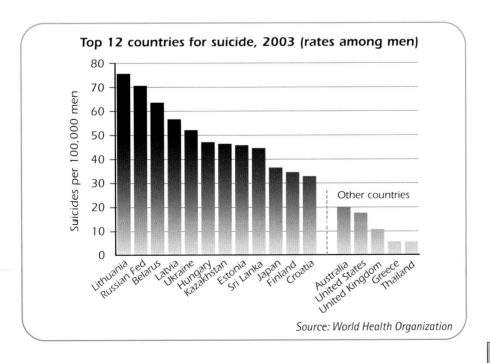

Top 12 countries for suicide, 2003 (rates among men)

Suicides per 100,000 men

Lithuania, Russian Fed, Belarus, Latvia, Ukraine, Hungary, Kazakhstan, Estonia, Sri Lanka, Japan, Finland, Croatia

Other countries: Australia, United States, United Kingdom, Greece, Thailand

Source: World Health Organization

Fertility and sexual health

Most women are thrilled to have a baby. However, for many of them, this also poses great danger. In the developing world, 500,000 women die as a result of pregnancy and childbirth each year, and 15 million more suffer serious, long-term health problems. Women in sub-Saharan Africa have a one in 13 chance of dying—compared with only one in 4,085 for women in the developed world. Many of these deaths are due to hemorrhaging, infections, and women being poorly nourished or giving birth too young.

SAVING MOTHERS, SAVING FAMILIES

Providing women in poorer countries with education can prevent many needless deaths. Educated women often marry later, may have a job, and

understand more about their health. They can learn about **contraception** and often choose to have fewer children. Condoms can also protect them against deadly diseases such as AIDS. When birth rates fall and more working mothers survive, families can spend more money on each child's food, health care, and schooling —meaning more children also survive.

Despite its one-child policy, China's population will continue growing to 1.5 billion before it starts to stabilize around 2025.

WHAT DO YOU THINK?
Should countries with high birth rates force people to have fewer children?

- Yes. China's population was growing out of control in the 1970s. A "one-child policy" saw the birth rate fall from 5.9 per woman in 1960 to 1.8 today, and people are much better-off.
- No. The policy involved forced abortions and heavy fines. Many Chinese people prefer a son and may abort female babies to try again for a boy. Males now outnumber females by 60 million. Neighboring India's birth rate has fallen from 5.8 to 3.2 through education alone.

However, declining birth rates can sometimes cause problems. In some developed countries, women now have so few children that populations are falling. Japanese women have only 1.3 children each on average and the population is expected to fall from 127 million today to 90 million by 2050. The Italian government, meanwhile, is offering women cash to have babies! A falling birth rate means fewer, younger workers to pay the health and social security bills of a growing elderly population.

A DANGEROUS GAME

Young people today are starting to have sex earlier and earlier. One million teenagers become pregnant each year worldwide, usually because they did not practice safe sex (use a condom). Sexually-transmitted diseases (STDs) —some of which can kill—are also a danger for teenagers who have unsafe sex. These include AIDS, **syphilis,** and **gonorrhea.** Chlamydia, an infection causing infertility, now affects one in nine UK teenagers and most cases of cervical cancer are caused by a sexually transmitted virus.

In the developed world, STDs among teenagers are most common in the United States, where young people generally receive less sex education than in Europe and Australia. The only 100 percent safe way of avoiding pregnancy and STDs is to not have sex.

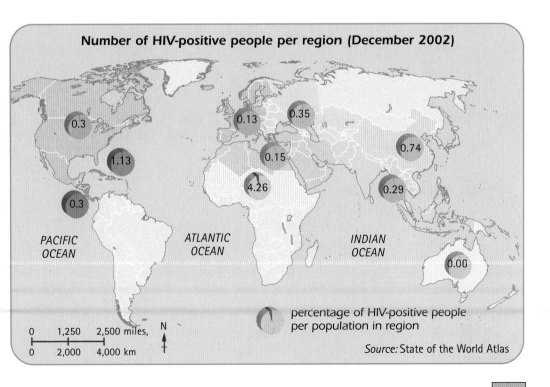

Number of HIV-positive people per region (December 2002)

0.3 0.13 0.35
1.13 0.15 0.74
0.3 4.26 0.29
0.00

PACIFIC OCEAN   ATLANTIC OCEAN   INDIAN OCEAN

percentage of HIV-positive people per population in region

| 0 | 1,250 | 2,500 miles, |
| 0 | 2,000 | 4,000 km |

N

Source: State of the World Atlas

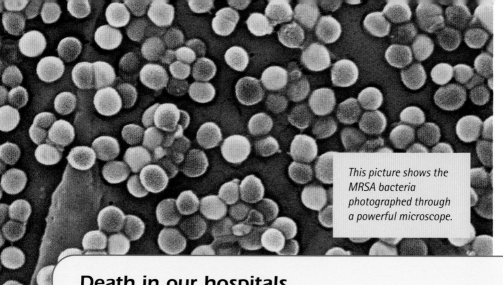

This picture shows the MRSA bacteria photographed through a powerful microscope.

Death in our hospitals

MRSA (methicillin-resistant *Staphylococcus aureus*) is harmless to healthy people, but can cause deadly fever and pneumonia in the sick or elderly, who often pick it up in the hospital. MRSA is now resistant to many antibiotics. In the United States, France, and Japan it is even resistant to vancomycin—traditionally regarded as "the last line of defense." Deaths from this "superbug" in England and Wales rose from 51 in 1993 to 800 in 2002. In the days before antibiotics, hospitals were kept much cleaner to prevent such bacterial outbreaks. Scientists are now testing a new double antibiotic, which they hope will be harder for MRSA to beat— at least for the time being.

Superbugs and antibacterial resistance

When the first antibiotics were developed around 50 years ago, people called them "wonder drugs." Until then, millions had regularly died from pneumonia or bacterial infections following injuries or childbirth.

THE BUGS FIGHT BACK

However, bacteria, which have been around for 3.5 billion years (human beings have existed for just 100,000 years), are already managing to beat our drugs.

The DNA of bacteria, like that of all living things, **mutates** as they reproduce. Some of these changes help them to survive antibiotics, and this **resistance** is passed on to their offspring. As bacteria can reproduce every 20 minutes, resistance develops very quickly.

THE HUMAN FACTOR

Antibiotics are supposed to be taken for a certain period of time to ensure that all the bacteria are killed. However, some people stop a course of antibiotics as soon as they feel better, or because they cannot afford to buy more. Others overuse them. Children in the Philippines are given antibiotics as "vitamins for the lungs," while in the West we unknowingly consume large amounts of them when we eat milk and meat. This is because farmers feed antibiotics to their livestock to keep them healthy and make them grow fast. Unfortunately, misusing antibiotics in these ways often strengthens, rather than destroys, the germs in our bodies.

What can you do?

- Always finish antibiotics, even if you no longer feel sick.
- Remember it is useless—and can even be dangerous—to take antibiotics for viral illnesses, such as colds or the flu.

A NEW PLAGUE?

Antibiotics are becoming increasingly useless against tuberculosis, with 425,000 drug-resistant cases developing each year. Death rates from drug-resistant TB are about 50 percent—double those of another bacterial plague, the Black Death, which devastated Medieval Europe.

HIV sufferers are at very high risk of getting and passing on TB (by coughing) to the rest of society. With around 45 million new HIV infections expected by 2010, some people fear drug-resistant TB could become a modern-day plague to rival the Black Death.

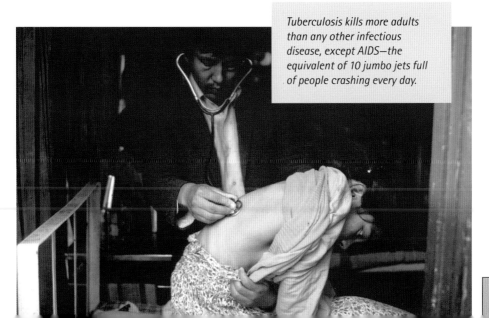

Tuberculosis kills more adults than any other infectious disease, except AIDS—the equivalent of 10 jumbo jets full of people crashing every day.

The global spread of viruses

Some of the world's newest, deadliest, diseases have been caused by viruses—for example, SARS (Severe Acute Respiratory Syndrome), AIDS, and most recently, bird flu.

Viruses are so tiny that 25 trillion (25,000,000,000,000) of them would fit on a pinhead. They infect every living thing—even bacteria. Antibiotics have no effect on viruses. Vaccinations can stop us from getting a viral disease—for example, polio or measles—in the first place, and antiviral drugs may help to reduce the effects of viruses. Other than that, however, our bodies must usually fight off viruses alone.

HIGH-SPEED TRAVELERS

Viruses can travel across the globe very quickly. The Spanish Flu, which killed up to 50 million people in 1918, spread around the world in just three months—at a time when few people traveled overseas. Today, 1.4 billion people travel by plane each year. Passengers can board planes before they start to feel sick, spreading diseases worldwide within hours.

SARS arrived in Hong Kong in February 2003, after an infected doctor traveled there from Guangdong in China. Before developing obvious symptoms himself, the doctor infected several guests in the hotel where he was staying—who then took the disease to Canada, Singapore, and Vietnam as they flew home. In total, 298 people died during the Hong Kong SARS outbreak.

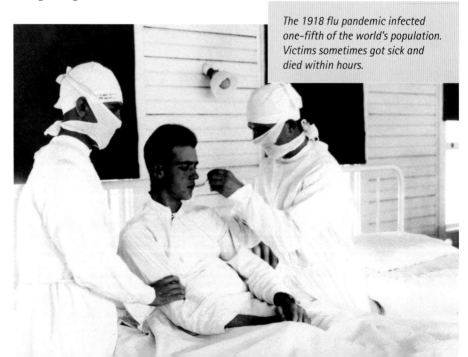

The 1918 flu pandemic infected one-fifth of the world's population. Victims sometimes got sick and died within hours.

Salesmen inspect a chicken at a poultry market in China, where millions of birds have been slaughtered to stop bird flu from spreading.

JUMPING THE SPECIES BARRIER

Many human viral diseases came from animals. HIV, for example, almost certainly spread to people from monkeys, eaten as a delicacy in West Africa. SARS, which terrorized China in 2003, came from civet cats, a wild animal eaten in exotic restaurants. These viruses were pretty harmless in their animal hosts—but became much more deadly once they mutated to infect humans. Today, a new kind of flu, H5N1, has spread to people from birds. Scientists fear a major pandemic might happen.

Bird flu has already affected more than 100 people in Asia since 1997, killing around 70 percent of them, often within 48 hours. Nearly all the victims were infected after handling dead or sick chickens. However, the virus may mutate to spread directly from human to human. It would then spread quickly through coughing. Although scientists would be able to create a vaccine, they would have to wait for the pandemic to start in order to obtain samples of the mutated virus. Millions could die during this delay.

What can you do?

- Don't panic—there is no immediate risk from bird flu, and scientists disagree on the likelihood of such diseases mutating to infect humans.
- To avoid infection with viruses (and bacteria, too), always wash your hands thoroughly and cook food well, especially meat.
- If you have a virus, drink plenty of water, rest, and stay at home to avoid infecting others.

Disease and the environment

Our food, water, and air are becoming increasingly polluted with industrially produced chemicals, many of them dangerous to our health. Around 80,000 of them, used in food, cosmetics, paints, plastics, fuels, and pesticides, have been created in the last 50 years alone.

We all have some of them in us. Even Inuit people living in the Arctic, thousands of miles away from the nearest factories, have extremely high levels of cancer-causing chemicals called PCBs in their blood. Although banned in the 1970s, PCBs have washed into the oceans, contaminating fish, whales, and seals—a large part of the Inuit diet.

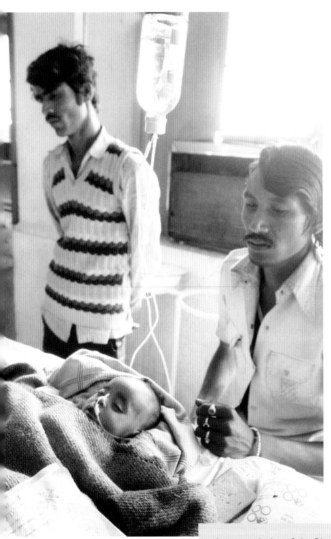

A young victim of the Bhopal leak in 1984 receives treatment in the hospital. Thousands of people were left blind or with breathing difficulties.

POISONOUS DISASTERS

Leaks of dangerous gases and chemicals used by industries can cause major health problems.

For example, a leak from an insecticide plant in Bhopal, India, in 1984 killed 4,000 people. It has since disabled tens of thousands more, while hundreds of people have suffered from cancer since the world's worst nuclear accident at Chernobyl, Ukraine, in 1986.

A BAD CLIMATE FOR HEALTH

Climate change will probably make temperatures more comfortable for disease-bearing insects. **West Nile virus**, carried by mosquitoes and originating in Africa, reached the United States in 1999, while malaria may one day return to southern Europe.

Vanishing wonder drugs

Many of today's most exciting new medicines come from rain forest plants. The rosy periwinkle flower from Madagascar, for example, is used to treat some cancers, while a liana (climbing plant) from Cameroon called *Ancistrocladus korupensis* may be able to fight AIDS. However, the world's rain forests are being chopped down at an alarming rate for timber and to make way for agriculture, and 80 percent have been destroyed already. Hundreds of plant and animal species are being made extinct each day—often before scientists have even discovered them. It is likely that we may already have lost cures for some of our deadliest diseases.

Climate change will also increase extreme weather events, such as the 2003 heatwave in France, when 10,000 elderly people died in temperatures above 104°F (40°C). Major storms, such as Hurricane Katrina in the United States in 2005, may cause infectious disease outbreaks by contaminating water supplies. Meanwhile, two-thirds of the world will not have enough water by 2025. This will cause disease and leave many regions unable to grow enough food.

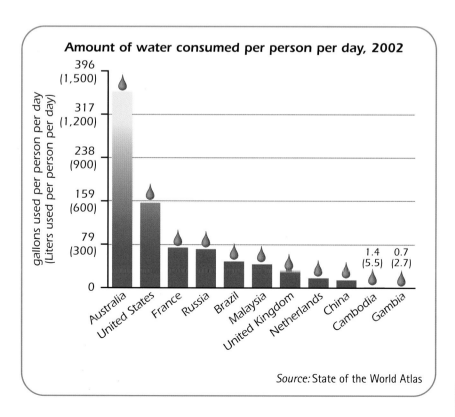

Source: State of the World Atlas

Debates About Health and Disease

The future of health—science fiction or salvation?

Some of today's most fascinating medical research seems like something from a science fiction movie. However, these techniques could change human health dramatically, maybe within as little as 10 years.

CLONING

Reproductive cloning takes DNA from a cell and uses it to create another genetically-identical animal—potentially creating animals to produce drugs, provide organs for human transplant, or to study human diseases. Cloning is still very difficult, though. The first clone, Dolly the sheep, took scientists 276 attempts, and many animals cloned so far have suffered serious health disorders.

Therapeutic cloning clones human embryos in order to harvest their stem cells, which can be programmed to become any of the body's other cells. These could be used to produce whole transplant organs from just one cell, or to replace damaged cells in people suffering from diseases such as **Alzheimer's** or **Parkinson's**, which kill tens of thousands of people every day.

Gene therapy could one day cure some of humanity's most distressing diseases—but much more research is needed to make sure it is safe.

Therapeutic cloning destroys the embryo—a potential human life—so some people see it as murder. Research is currently only allowed in a few countries.

NANOMEDICINE

Today's diseases could be made a thing of the past by nanomedicine. Mini biological machines, three-billionths of a foot (one-billionth of a meter) wide, and too small to be seen with a conventional microscope, would swim through our blood to fix damaged cells, pump life-saving medicines into precise target areas, or search out and destroy early cancer cells.

These five piglets were cloned at a laboratory in the United States. Other animals cloned so far include cattle, mice, and dogs.

More research is needed to prove that substances in the blood will not stick to these nanoparticles, triggering unintended effects such as blood clotting, and that damaging toxic materials will not "piggyback" their way into cells along with the tiny machines.

GENE THERAPY

Gene therapy could replace abnormal genes that cause diseases such as cystic fibrosis, sickle cell anemia, and **Huntington's disease**, with normal, healthy genes. This could be done using deactivated viruses to "infect" patients' cells, delivering the genes to their target. So far, however, trials have proved extremely expensive and difficult, with one patient dying and others getting sick. There are also concerns about using gene therapy to alter egg or sperm cells, which would mean the changed genes being passed on to future generations—rather than just treating individual patients.

CRYONICS

Around 100 dead people have already been **cryonically** frozen, and more than 800 have each paid $30,000 to be frozen when they die. They hope that technology in future centuries can revive them and cure whatever caused their death—an "ambulance to the future."

There are some concerns, though, that people in the future may not bother to revive those frozen centuries before, and that revived patients could be exploited as medical curiosities, would not be legally alive, and may suffer severe depression.

Most of the millions of animals killed in medical experiments each year are mice and rats.

Should we test medicines on animals?

All medicines are tested on animals to prove they work and are safe—but many animals suffer pain and some are killed as part of these tests. Some people feel such experiments are cruel, but many others are strongly in favor of them, as they have led to the development of antibiotics, vaccines, and treatments for illnesses such as diabetes and heart disease.

FURTHER APART THAN WE THOUGHT?

Animal testing is not perfect due to important differences between humans and animals. Despite decades of animal testing, we still cannot cure many common diseases.

Genetic conditions, such as cystic fibrosis, are caused by faults in just one nucleotide (the building blocks of DNA). Although we share 98 percent of our genes with chimpanzees, the remaining 2 percent contains 60 million different nucleotides. Drugs can also have different effects on different species. We would never have penicillin (the world's most commonly used antibiotic) if it had been tested on guinea pigs, because it kills them.

Animals are often used to test treatments for diseases—such as Parkinson's or Alzheimer's—which they do not naturally suffer from. Scientists artificially induce the symptoms, which may not develop or respond in the same way as the human disease. Animal tests may not entirely guarantee a drug's safety, either. Around 100,000 deaths each year in the United States are caused by side effects to new drugs.

People against animal experiments believe the only useful and safe way to test new drugs is on human volunteers and human tissues, and with computer modeling. They believe the millions spent on animal tests should be devoted to funding better public health education, to prevent many diseases from developing in the first place.

BEING CRUEL TO BE KIND

Most scientists agree that animal tests are far from perfect, but say human lives must come before animal lives in the battle against disease.

A cell culture grown in a test tube cannot yet give results as useful as a whole animal, and if drugs went on sale without animal testing, the human deaths from side effects would be much higher. Animals have also benefited from animal experimentation—as a result of these tests, we have drugs to treat our pets when they are sick.

Controls introduced in Western countries now ensure laboratory animals live in better conditions, suffer less pain, and that as few animals as possible are used. If animal experimentation was banned in the West, it would still have to be done somewhere to ensure drugs meet safety requirements— probably in countries with few or no animal welfare laws at all.

While no one likes to see animals suffer, it seems that animal experimentation will be with us for many years to come.

Animal experiments have helped scientists to develop the drugs to treat many serious diseases.

The health of the poor in the hands of multinationals

Around $100 billion is spent on health research globally every year—but only 10 percent of this money is devoted to 90 percent of the world's health problems. This so-called "10-90 Gap" exists because many diseases are not profitable to pharmaceutical research companies. For example, while many expensive treatments for obesity, sleeping, and sexual problems have come onto the market over the past five years, none of the big drug companies has developed any treatments for **Chagas disease**, which kills 50,000 people per year, or **leishmaniasis**, which kills 200,000.

This is because these diseases mainly affect poor people in the developing world, who would not be able to afford medicines were they to be developed. Nearly all research funding for these diseases has come from wealthy donors, such as Microsoft founder Bill Gates.

Scientists say cures for some diseases, such as malaria—which kills more than two million people per year—could probably be developed quickly if funds were available.

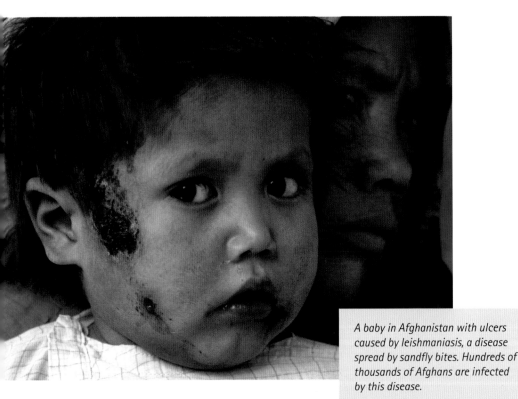

A baby in Afghanistan with ulcers caused by leishmaniasis, a disease spread by sandfly bites. Hundreds of thousands of Afghans are infected by this disease.

An inhumane industry?

Almost 40 pharmaceutical companies took the South African government to court in 2001 (they later dropped their case) to stop it from allowing the manufacture and import of cheaper versions of their expensive AIDS drugs, which keep sufferers in the West alive indefinitely. In Africa, the disease is a death sentence for millions of poor people.

However, the drugs companies insist they acted not out of cruelty, but principle. The patents system, designed to protect inventions for 20 years or more, stops people from copying drugs and selling them as cheaper alternatives—something that happens regularly in India and parts of Africa, which have still not signed international patent protection laws.

It takes pharmaceutical companies between 10 to 15 years, and costs more than $500 million, to create each new drug. Patent breakers—who themselves do no research—can copy the drug for less than 1 percent of this cost.

Pharmaceutical companies say that if they cannot be sure their profits will be protected, they may no longer be able to devote years of research into important diseases.

Protestors march in South Africa to demand that HIV-positive people are given the drugs that could save their lives.

AN IMPOSSIBLE SITUATION?

Poor people need cheap drugs, but we all need research to find new treatments for diseases such as cancer. A solution is needed so drug companies can still make a profit, while disease sufferers in the developing world can afford medicines

This could involve giving companies a financial reward for their discoveries, and then immediately allowing the drugs to be copied. However, this is very unpopular among pharmaceutical companies. The right solution could still be a long way off.

What's the Outlook?

In 2000, the United Nations set out its Millennium Development Goals for 2015, many aimed at improving health in the developing world, including:
• cutting child deaths from preventable illnesses by two-thirds;
• halting and beginning to reverse malaria, TB, and AIDS;
• halving the number of people without access to safe drinking water;
• reducing the numbers of women dying during childbirth by 75 percent.
However, with shortages of doctors, poor health services, and lack of funding in the developing world, these important targets will be hard to meet.

So far, little progress has been made in cutting child deaths, with 11 million under five years old still dying annually worldwide, up to 40 percent of them in sub-Saharan Africa.

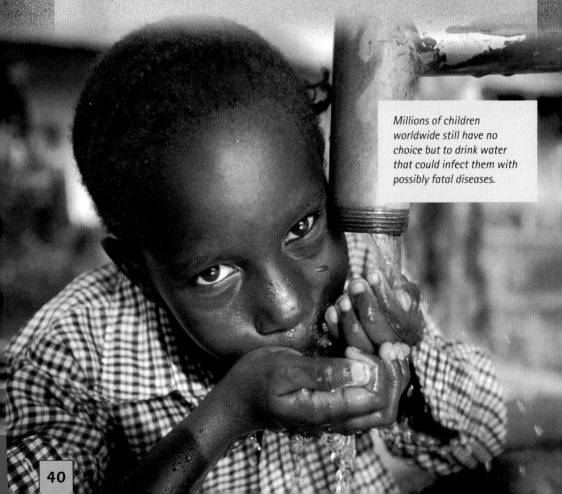

Millions of children worldwide still have no choice but to drink water that could infect them with possibly fatal diseases.

MORE HELP NEEDED

In 2005, the G8 (a group of the world's richest developed countries) promised funding to fully wipe out polio—originally a target for 2000. They gave an extra $50 billion of aid to the developing world, and wrote off 18 of the poorest countries' debts. However, some people claim that giving aid to the developing world has little effect on health there, and may even make governments less likely to help their own people.

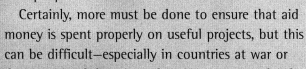

Wealthy countries, such as the G8, must work together to overcome health problems in the developing world.

Certainly, more must be done to ensure that aid money is spent properly on useful projects, but this can be difficult—especially in countries at war or during natural disasters, when innocent people's health suffers most.

Health aid will be needed more, rather than less, in the future, as AIDS continues to ravage the developing world, and climate change causes more droughts and disasters, leaving large parts of the world with less food and water than ever.

EDUCATION AND VACCINATION

As populations grow and age, health costs for governments will also grow. Public awareness campaigns will be urgently needed to help prevent diseases that cost millions to treat, including HIV and those caused by smoking and poor diet. Research to develop new vaccines against AIDS and malaria will be a major priority, as will increasing the developing world's access to already-existing vaccines to fight other killer diseases, including measles and tetanus. Perhaps the world's most urgent health challenge is a possible bird flu pandemic. However, only 20 percent of countries have yet drawn up emergency plans, and even fewer are stockpiling antiviral drugs to help treat the sick before a vaccine is developed.

TIME FOR ACTION

Wealthy countries can help to close the world's huge health gaps—but this will mean providing money, expert advice, and hard work over many years. Short-lived media campaigns cannot solve the problems that have led to the world's richest people now living twice as long as the poorest.

Statistical Information

Major causes of death worldwide

Most deaths from non-infectious diseases today are in the developed world, although this is set to change soon as developing countries urbanize.

Disease	Percentage of total deaths
Heart disease (non-infectious)	39.3
Infectious and parasitic diseases (infectious)	19.3
Cancer (non-infectious)	12.6
Injuries	9.0
Respiratory infections (infectious)	7.0
Others	7.0
Respiratory diseases (non-infectious)	6.3
Conditions of pregnancy, birth, infancy	4.4
Digestive diseases (non-infectious)	3.5

Source: World Health Organization

Government per capita spending on health care (2002)

The World Health Organization recommends around $30–40 per person per year. The U.S. figures are high, despite the lack of a general national health system, because of heavy spending on programs such as Medicare (which provides health care for people aged over 65) and health assistance for military veterans and indigenous peoples.

Country	Amount in dollars per person
United States	2,368
France	1,786
United Kingdom	1,693
Canada	1,552
Greece	634
Hungary	496
Algeria	57
Morocco	55
China	21
Mali	12
Zambia	11

Source: World Health Organization

Births with a skilled attendant

Having a skilled doctor or midwife present during a birth can mean the difference between life and death for a mother and her baby. While women in developed countries can normally rely on having a trained professional to help them, this is not the case in many of the world's countries.

Country	Percentage of births with skilled attendant
New Zealand (1995)	100.0
South Korea (1997)	100.0
Czech Republic (2002)	99.9
United Kingdom (1998)	99.0
United States (2001)	99.0
Malaysia (2002)	97.0
Mexico (1997)	85.7
Vietnam (2002)	85.0
Turkey (1998)	83.0
Indonesia (2003)	66.3
Bolivia (2002)	65.1
Gambia (2000)	54.7
Cambodia (2000)	31.8
Pakistan (1998)	20.0
Afghanistan (2003)	14.0
Bangladesh (2003)	13.9
Ethiopia (2000)	5.6

Source: World Health Organization
year = most recent data available

Percentage increase in world's urban populations by 2015

Africa	71
Asia	46
Latin America & Caribbean	30
North America	19
Oceania	15
Europe	1

Source: The State of the World Atlas, *2003*

Percentage of adults without access to clean water supply (2000)

Ethiopia	76
Cambodia	70
Angola	62
Haiti	54
Jamaica	29
China	25
Indonesia	24
Peru	23
Mexico	14
India	12
Cuba	5
Egypt	5

Source: The State of the World Atlas, *2003*

Infant mortality rate per 1,000 live births (2000)

Sierra Leone	180
Afghanistan	165
Niger	159
Zimbabwe	73
Guatemala	44
China	32
Lebanon	28
Venezuela	20
Argentina	18
Bulgaria	15
Cuba	7
United States	6.5
Belgium	6
United Kingdom	5

Source: The State of the World Atlas, *2003*

Glossary

acupuncture Chinese medicine that inserts fine needles into the skin

AIDS (Acquired Immune Deficiency Syndrome) disease that develops after infection with HIV

Alzheimer's disease disease that causes memory loss, speech loss, and personality changes in the elderly

anemia lack of red blood cells, causing weakness, and lack of energy

autopsy medical examination of a dead body to determine the cause of death

ayurveda Indian medicine based upon holy texts, herbal remedies, and diet

bacteria microscopic organisms, the most numerous life forms on Earth

CFCs (chlorofluorocarbons) chemicals used in refrigerators, solvents, and aerosols that destroy the ozone layer. They are now banned in many countries.

Chagas disease occurring only in the Americas and spread through insect bites. People often die years later from nerve, heart, or digestive problems.

cholera bacterial infection spread through dirty water, causing massive diarrhea, vomiting, and often death from dehydration

cirrhosis condition where the liver becomes scarred, filled with fat, and eventually stops working

communism system of government in which the state controls the economy

contraception use of products such as condoms or the Pill to stop a woman from becoming pregnant

cryonics freezing of a dead person. The body is preserved until medical cures can bring the person back to life.

cystic fibrosis genetic illness causing severe breathing difficulties and early death

dehydration loss of water and important blood salts, which can stop the body's organs from working

depression common mental health condition, which can range from persistent sadness to suicidal thoughts

DNA deoxyribonucleic acid, which contains the genetic code for most life forms

GDP (Gross Domestic Product) size of a country's economy

genes information passing on characteristics from parents to children, such as eye color

gonorrhea sexually transmitted bacterial infection that can cause infertility in women

hemorrhage uncontrollable bleeding

HIV (Human Immunodeficiency Virus) virus that causes AIDS, often spread through sex and by drug users sharing needles

HIV/AIDS term used to describe all stages from infection with HIV to development of AIDS, which may take many years

Huntington's disease genetic disease that destroys nerves, causing jerky movements and mental deterioration

immune resistant to an infectious disease

leishmaniasis often fatal parasitic disease spread by sandfly bites

mutate change the genetic material of a cell

nomadic communities that move from place to place

obese being so overweight that it affects your health

Parkinson's disease disease that destroys brain cells, causing trembling of muscles and affecting speech and balance

pneumonia inflammation of the lungs, often caused by bacteria

polio viral disease causing paralysis

resistance ability of an organism to withstand attacks by disease

schizophrenia mental illness causing distorted thinking, hallucinations, and inability to feel normal emotions

Soviet Union political union between Russia and a group of other communist countries, that lasted from 1922 to 1991

syphilis sexually transmitted bacterial infection that has mild early symptoms, but can cause mental deterioration and death

tuberculosis (TB) bacterial disease that can infect many organs, usually the lungs. Without treatment, sufferers generally die.

typhoid potentially fatal bacterial disease spread through dirty food and water

virus microscopic organism not technically alive that breaks into living cells in order to reproduce, causing illness

West Nile virus mosquito-spread disease. Most people have only mild symptoms, but some may suffer coma, paralysis, and death.

Further Information

Books

Children in Crisis series (World Almanac Library, 2005) This six-book series provides the real stories of six young people surviving in difficult circumstances, often affecting their health, with titles including: *Living as a Child Laborer, Living in a Refugee Camp*, and *Living with AIDS*.

Cobain, Bev. *When Nothing Matters Anymore: A Survival Guide for Depressed Teens* (Free Spirit Publishing, 1998) The cousin of Nirvana singer Kurt Cobain, who committed suicide in 1994, provides facts, clears up misconceptions, discusses warning signs, and provides treatment options for depression, addictions, eating disorders, and suicide attempts.

Ingram, Scott. *Want Fries With That?: Obesity And The Supersizing Of America* (Franklin Watts, 2005) America's obesity epidemic is tackled here, using statistics and scientific research, and also looking at the social and health impacts of obesity, and issues such as advertising and the availability of fast food.

Smith, Dan. *The State of the World Atlas* (Earthscan, 2003) A reference book using maps and graphics to present some of the most important issues affecting the world today, with a section on Health and Disease and related sections, including Urbanization, Global Warming, and Traffic.

Townsend, John. *A Painful History of Medicine* series (Raintree, 2005) A graphically illustrated series looking at the history of health and disease, with intriguing titles such as *Scalpels, Stitches, and Scars* and *Bedpans, Blood, and Bandages*.

Websites

UNICEF (United Nations Children's Fund)
www.unicef.org/
This site explains many of the issues affecting children's health in the developing world, for example droughts, natural disasters, AIDS, unsafe drinking water, immunization, and education.

ORBIS
http://www.orbis.org/
Gives much information about blindness and vision problems in the developing world—and programs to help affected people.

WHO (the World Health Organization)
www.who.int
Gives lots of information on specific countries—life expectancy, amount spent by governments on health care, etc. It also provides information on specific health issues and problems.

Millennium Development Goals
www.un.org/millenniumgoals
Information on the eight goals, which range from halving extreme poverty to halting the spread of HIV/AIDS and providing universal primary education, all by the target date of 2015.

Samaritans
www.samaritans.org
Samaritans is a 24 hour-a-day service providing confidential emotional support for people who are experiencing depression or feeling suicidal.

Madre
www.madre.org
This NGO works to promote human rights in the developing world. It will deliver spare medical supplies to people in need in Iraq, Kenya, Palestine, Rwanda, Cuba, and many other countries in Latin America.

Contact addresses

American Red Cross
National Headquarters
2025 E Street, NW
Washington, DC 20006

UNICEF (United States)
UNICEF House
3 United Nations Plaza
New York, New York 10017

ORBIS International
520 8th Avenue
11th Floor
New York, New York 10018

INDEX